Bojo the Hippo

To THE BEST!

J. Donnison

Written & Illustrated

by J. DONNISON

WHITEHIPPOUSA

ISBN-13: 978-1986239899
ISBN-10: 1986239896

It was a mostly normal day at Nanny Franny's Stuffed Animal Factory, until Jimmy noticed a little stuffed hippo was mixed up with the stuffed bears.

"How in the world did this *happy hippo* get mixed up with the *smiling bears?*" Jimmy wondered to himself.

Jimmy called over the factory supervisor, Miss Kathy, and asked her if she happened to know how the little hippo got mixed up with the bears.

"Oh, that's Bojo the Hippo," Miss Kathy explained. "But I'm not sure how he got mixed up with the bears. Why don't you just throw him over with the other stuffed animals that need mending and I'll sort him out later."

"Yes, ma'am!" Jimmy said with a smile.

Jimmy threw Bojo just as Miss Kathy had instructed, but he missed his mark... Badly.

"Oh no, Jimmy!" Miss Kathy cried out. "You threw Bojo, *right out the window!*"

"*Wooooooooooowww!!!*" Bojo howled as he sailed out the window. A bit of luck and a strong gust of wind sent Bojo flying further than any stuffed hippo had ever flown before.

"Go, hippo! Go!" Jimmy shouted from the window. "Look at that little stuffed hippo go!"

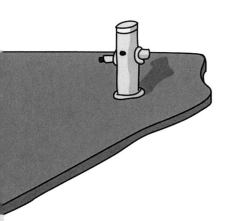

Across the street and down the way, local tennis star Anna O. and her grandfather, Grampa O., were just leaving Yo-Yo's Sporting Emporium with a brand new tennis racket, when Bojo came sailing directly towards them. Without a thought about it, Anna swung her new racket... *WHACK!*

"Wow! Great shot, Anna!" Grampa O. cheered. "Oh, my. That little guy sure can fly!"

Three blocks over, the guys from Jumpin' Joe's Trampolines were making a delivery when Bojo came flying in... *BOING!* Bojo bounced higher and further than any stuffed hippo had ever bounced before!

Down the street and up the road, Hank "the Hayman" was heading out to farm country when Bojo came crashing down in the back of the Hayman's hay truck.

"Hey, man. Who's back there?" the Hayman muttered to himself. Bojo was in no condition to introduce himself to the Hayman. All that flying and bouncing and crashing around town made the little stuffed hippo quite dizzy.

Once his dizziness was gone and forgotten, Bojo realized he rather enjoyed riding in the back of the Hayman's hay truck. With the wind in his face and the wonderful sights and sounds of nature all about, Bojo was as happy as a little stuffed hippo could be.

"Hello, friends!" Bojo shouted to the animals as he and the Hayman drove along. "They sure don't have animals like you guys back at the factory."

Bojo was awfully distracted by all the lovely nature he and the Hayman were driving past. The little stuffed hippo did not even notice a great bald eagle was swooping in, *directly for him...*

In the blink of an eye, the great bald eagle snatched Bojo from the back of the Hayman's hay truck. "Hey, man," was all the Hayman could say, as he watched Bojo and the bald eagle fly further and further away. "Put me down!" Bojo shouted at the eagle. "I'm not food! I'm Bojo!"

"This is amazing!!!" Bojo exclaimed as he and the eagle soared
higher and higher. Bojo enjoyed flying high with the eagle very much.
What Bojo did not enjoy was the eagle mistaking him for food... *CHOMP!*

"Yuck!" the eagle screamed. "You're not food! You're not food at all! To the forest floor with you!"

"I told you I wasn't *foooooooood!!!*" Bojo replied as he fell from the sky.

Bojo's crash landing onto the forest floor caused a commotion that was heard by nearly all the animals in the forest.

"Oh my aching, dizzy head," Bojo groaned.

Luckily, Shnacks the Fox and his dear friend, Albin the Owl were nearby when Bojo came crashing down.

"Get your supplies, Albin," Shnacks said quickly. "This little guy needs our help!"

Shnacks and Albin knew every animal in the forest but they had never seen an animal like Bojo the Hippo before. Shnacks grabbed a piece of Bojo's stuffing and gave it a close look. *"What is this stuff?"* Shnacks wondered aloud. "Say, what kind of animal are you anyway?"

"That stuff is *stuffing!*" Albin answered correctly. "So I suppose that makes this little guy a *stuffed animal.*"

Bojo was growing nervous.

"Don't worry little guy," Albin said assuringly to Bojo. "You just need a bit of mending and I think I just might have the supplies to do the job!"

Albin opened his supply kit but it was nearly empty.

"My word, Albin," Shnacks gasped. "Your supply kit is in desperate need of more supplies!"

"Yikes," Albin grimaced. "I guess I don't have the supplies to do the job."

"Well, we better think of something, *fast!*" Shnacks said sharply. "Our stuffed friend here needs some fixing and if we can't do it, we better think of someone who can!"

After a moment of thinking Shnacks snapped his fingers and exclaimed, "I got it! The family in the tall house from way down the way that's actually not too far away at all!"

"Shnacks, you clever fox, that's a great idea!" Albin said with a smile. "The family in the tall house are great people! I've seen them be nice to animals. I bet they are nice to *stuffed animals too!* We shall leave at once!"

"Thank you friends," Bojo said to Shnacks and Albin. "You really are the kindest fox and owl I have ever known."

With just three flaps of his wings, Albin and Bojo were on their way. "Good-bye and good luck, my little stuffed hippo friend!" Shnacks howled as he waved farewell.

After a short flight over the hills and down the way, Albin and Bojo reached their destination. "There they are," Albin cheered when he saw Sammy and his father, Mr. Greeny. "I'll fly a bit closer and drop you in for a safe landing. I hope they can catch."

"Bye-bye little stuffed hippo," Albin said as he released Bojo. "I'll visit you soon enough my friend."

"Thanks again, Albin!" Bojo hollered back as he fell toward Sammy and Mr. Greeny. "You truly are the most wonderful owl I have ever known."

As Albin flew back to the forest, Sammy and his father marveled at their catch.

"Look Dad! It's a little stuffed hippo," Sammy told his father. "But I think he's hurt. He needs our help!"

"You're right, Sammy," Mr. Greeny said. "Looks like this little guy has had quite an adventure. Let's get him home for some much needed mending."

Once home, Sammy quickly gathered all the supplies he could find. "A pointy needle, a bit of strong thread, and some careful sewing should fix this little stuffed hippo right up!"

"What's all the hubbub about?" Sammy's mother asked when she walked in the room.

While his parents chatted away, Sammy carefully sewed the tear in Bojo's side. "There you go little guy," Sammy said with a smile. "One more stitch and you'll be as good as new!"

Bojo was as grateful and happy as a little stuffed hippo could be.

Three stitches later, Sammy declared, "You're all healed up little friend!"

Bojo burst into Sammy's arms. "Thank you Sammy," Bojo said as he hugged his new best friend. "You've made me the happiest little stuffed hippo in the whole world!"

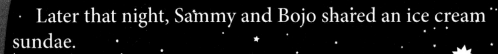

Later that night, Sammy and Bojo shared an ice cream sundae.

"I always enjoy an ice cream sundae after a good adventure," Sammy told Bojo.

"Me too!" the happy hippo replied. "Sammy, do you think we will go on many adventures together?" Bojo wondered.

"Well of course we will," Sammy assured Bojo. "That's what best friends do."

Bojo the Hippo ended his adventure filled day by Sammy's side, as he would, for many happy years to come.

The End

75345210R00020

Made in the USA
San Bernardino, CA
29 April 2018